M🌰USE SCOUTS

Make Friends

MOUSE SCOUTS

Make Friends

Sarah Dillard

Yearling | Knopf

Visit us on the Web! rhcbooks.com

Educators and librarians, for a variety of teaching tools, visit us at RHTeachersLibrarians.com

Library of Congress Cataloging-in-Publication Data
Names: Dillard, Sarah, author, illustrator.
Title: Make friends / Sarah Dillard.
Description: First edition. I New York : Alfred A. Knopf, [2018] I Series: Mouse Scouts ; 4 I Summary: "When Miss Poppy assigns the troop a new badge—Making Friends—the girls think it will be easy. They're already friends, so what more is there to do?! But when the Acorn Scouts learn they will need to team up with the boys in the Maple Scouts as part of the badge, everything changes." Provided by publisher
Identifiers: LCCN 2017038097 (print) I LCCN 2017022506 (ebook) I ISBN 978-0-385-75612-9 (pbk.) I ISBN 978-0-385-75614-3 (ebook)
Subjects: I CYAC: Scouting (Youth activity)—Fiction. I Friendship—Fiction. I Mice—Fiction. I BISAC: JUVENILE FICTION / Animals / General. I JUVENILE FICTION / Nature & the Natural World / General (see also headings under Animals). I JUVENILE FICTION / Family / General (see also headings under Social Issues).
Classification: LCC PZ7.D57733 (print) I LCC PZ7.D57733 Man 2018 (ebook) I DDC [Fic]—dc23

Printed in the United States of America
January 2018
10 9 8 7 6 5 4 3 2 1

First Edition

For Amy, Liza, and Tracey—
some friends I've made

Contents

CHAPTER 1

The "Make Friends" Badge

One day, Violet and Tigerlily were walking to their Mouse Scout meeting. Well, Violet was walking. Tigerlily jumped up into the hedge next to the sidewalk and began swinging from branch to branch. Violet didn't pay much attention. Tigerlily never walked if there was a more challenging route to take.

"I wonder what badge we'll be work-ing on next," Violet said. "I hope it's flower fashions!" The night before, Violet had thought of a way to make a tutu out of dandelion petals. She couldn't wait to try it. She did a little pirouette as she imag-ined how the dandelion petals would flutter.

Tigerlily gave a final swing from a branch and let go. She soared through the air and landed right in front of Violet. "Maybe it will be something fun, like building canoes," Tigerlily said.

"Whatever badge it is, I hope we have a good snack today!" Violet said.

"I'm in the mood-a for some Gouda!" Tigerlily said.

"Be a smarty. Eat Havarti!" Violet said. They giggled together the rest of their walk.

Violet and Tigerlily were the last Scouts to arrive at the meeting. They quickly joined the other girls in a circle on the floor. Soon they heard the shrill tweet of an emergency whistle. Miss Poppy had arrived. "QUIET, EVERYONE!" she bellowed. Then she looked at the Scouts and smiled.

"Today we are going to talk about friendship! What could be more special than having a good friend? Someone to share your feelings with. Someone to laugh with, someone to cry with, someone to talk to when you are lonely. *That* is what friendship is."

Violet looked around the room and felt a warm glow for her fellow Acorn Scouts.

She admired Junebug's intelligence and Cricket's kind heart. Petunia could always make her laugh, and even Hyacinth was nice when she wasn't so busy being perfect. And of course, she couldn't forget Tigerlily! There was no better friend in the world.

Miss Poppy became dreamy-eyed. "Why, I remember MY best friend and all the escapades we had when WE were Scouts.

In fact, there was this one time—" she chuckled, then stopped herself. "Well, we were young and silly. But the important thing is, we were good Scouts. That is all that matters."

The Mouse Scouts looked at their leader in awe. Miss Poppy—*young?* And the thought of her having a friend? It seemed impossible!

Petunia narrowed her eyes. "How come we've never heard of this friend?" she asked.

Miss Poppy smoothed her skirt and squared her shoulders. "That was another time and place," she said. "Now, then. If you haven't guessed, today we will start work on your 'Make Friends' badge!"

Violet felt a quick stab of disappointment. She had her heart set on making a dandelion tutu. *Oh well,* she thought. *I can always make it on my own.*

Tigerlily didn't mind. She knew all about friendship already, so she would have plenty of time left over to do something fun.

"This will be the easiest badge ever!" she said.

Just then Miss Poppy leaned forward, and her expression became serious.

"Remember: Friendship isn't all sunshine and giggles. It takes understanding, compassion, and respect. Sometimes you will have to think of your friend before you think of yourself. Sometimes you will disagree. Sometimes you might wonder why you were ever friends in the first place. Some friendships last forever, while others don't stand the test of time. To have a good friend, you have to be a good friend. And that can be hard work!"

Miss Poppy stopped and looked around the room. The Scouts looked at each other. Then Tigerlily laughed. "Don't

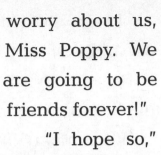

worry about us, Miss Poppy. We are going to be friends forever!"

"I hope so," said Miss Poppy. "For the next few weeks, we will work on our 'Make Friends' badges. Every day you will strive not only to be a good friend to those you know, but also to be friendly to someone you do *not* know. During this time, you will keep a friendship journal in which you will record your thoughts on friends and your efforts to be friendly. We will start today by making friendship bracelets, and at the end of the month, we will have a Celebration of Friendship."

The Scouts were beaming. Tigerlily was right; this badge was going to be a piece of cake! Then Miss Poppy cleared her throat.

"Oh, there is one more thing I forgot to mention," Miss Poppy said. "We will not be working on this badge on our own. The Maple Scouts are also working on their 'Make Friends' badges. They will be joining us at our next meeting to begin planning our Celebration of Friendship event . . . which we'll be doing together."

"The Maple Scouts?" Violet gasped. "But they're *boys*!"

But they're boys!

MOUSE SCOUT HANDBOOK

An Introduction to the "Make Friends" Badge

There is nothing more important to a Mouse
Scout than being a good friend. In fact, without
friendship, there would be no Mouse Scouts!
The organization was founded as a result of the
lifelong friendship between Daisy and Hydrangea. As you will remember, their friendship

began when Daisy, an intrepid field mouse, nursed Hydrangea, a house mouse who had been trapped and released in the wild, back to health.

Through the example set by Daisy and Hydrangea, Mouse Scouts strive to find common ground in friendships while also delighting in the differences that make each one of us unique.

Every Mouse Scout knows that if she approaches a new mouse as a potential *friend,* she will have few enemies.

~ ~

CHAPTER 2

Friendship Bracelets

Violet's nose twitched, and she grabbed
her tail. She did not want
anything to do with the
Maple Scouts. "We CAN'T
be friends with the Maple
Scouts!" she cried.

The other Scouts nodded
in agreement.

"I've heard they eat worms,"
said Cricket.

"They are very unsanitary," said Junebug.

"They have no social niceties," said Hyacinth.

"They are mean, horrible mice," said Petunia.

"We don't need any new friends!" said Tigerlily. "We have each other!"

Miss Poppy sighed. "Just try to keep an open mind, Acorns. They might surprise you. Now—let's get started on our friendship bracelets."

Miss Poppy handed out different-colored pieces of string. Each Scout got twelve pieces.

Miss Poppy cleared her throat and said, "You will make two bracelets. One to give to an old friend and one to give to a new friend."

"I'm not giving one to a Maple Scout!" Petunia said. The other Scouts giggled.

Miss Poppy narrowed her eyes and then went on. "The six pieces of string represent loyalty, trust, honesty, acceptance, generosity, and love—the six most important ingredients in friendship. The bracelets are made by twisting the six pieces of string together."

Miss Poppy smiled at the Scouts, and they all smiled back. Violet even forgot about the Maple Scouts for a moment. She couldn't wait to get started on her bracelets. She pulled her strings out straight and tied a knot in one end. Then she twisted the six strings together until they formed one string. *It's just like us,* she thought. *Six different friends, all together in one troop!* She was glad that she got to make a second bracelet, even though she couldn't imagine who she would give it to.

Tigerlily was having a hard time with her bracelet. She tied a knot at the end, but when she tried to twist the strings together, they just got tangled up. Some strands were loose, while others seemed to be too tight. *I don't know about friendship*, she thought, *but making this bracelet is not easy.* She spent more time on the second bracelet, but it was no better.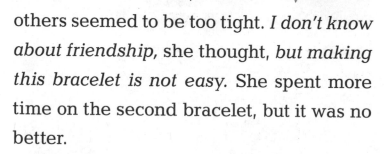

When they were finished, Miss Poppy told them to trade one of their bracelets with a friend. "The bracelet will always be a reminder to you that your friend is with you."

It was easy for Violet to decide who to

give her bracelet to. She turned to Tigerlily and tied it around her wrist.

Tigerlily looked at Violet's bracelet. It
was perfect. Tigerlily tied the one she
had made around Violet's wrist. It was
a little bit loose, and there were stray
pieces of string hanging out of it. Tigerlily
blushed. "Your bracelet turned out better,"
she said.

"That's okay," Violet said as she looked at the bracelet. "It's the friendship behind it that counts." The bracelet she had made for Tigerlily *was* much nicer. She wished Tigerlily had tried a little harder on the bracelet.

Hyacinth and Petunia were admiring their bracelets. "They look exactly alike!" Petunia said.

"Almost," said Hyacinth as she pulled at a loose string on the bracelet that Petunia had given her.

Junebug tied her bracelet around Cricket's wrist, but when Cricket went to tie hers around Junebug's wrist, Junebug asked her to put it on her sash instead. "Synthetic fibers give me a rash," she explained.

Miss Poppy called the Scouts to get their snacks. There were small squares of cheddar cheese, and raisins for Junebug, who was lactose-intolerant. The troop enjoyed the snacks and tried not to think about the worms that they would most likely have for snacks at the next meeting with the Maple Scouts.

Tigerlily looked over to make sure Miss Poppy wasn't paying attention. Then she leaned in and whispered, "The Maple

Scouts may be coming to our next meeting, but we don't have to make it easy for them."

"What can we do?" asked Violet. "If we don't work with them, we won't earn our badge, and Miss Poppy might send us back to Buttercups!"

"It might be better than having to work with the Maple Scouts!" said Petunia.

"I don't have a plan yet," said Tigerlily, "but let's all think about it tonight. Tomorrow we can meet in the park and decide what to do."

MOUSE SCOUT HANDBOOK

Friendship Bracelets

A friendship bracelet is a lovely token that one friend gives to another to commemorate their friendship. While you can buy a friendship bracelet, making them is fun, easy, and so much more meaningful.

There are many ways to make friendship bracelets. They may be woven, beaded, crocheted, knotted, or twisted. Here are instructions for a simple twisted bracelet.

1. Take six strands of string and lay them together.

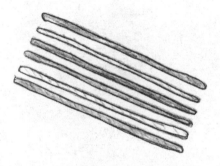

2. Tie a knot in one end. Hold the knotted end with one hand.

3. Grasp the unknotted ends of the strings with your other hand.

4. Slowly and tightly twist the strands together until they form a single rope.

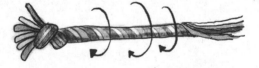

5. Tie a knot in the unknotted end of the single rope.

6. Tie your bracelet around the wrist of a friend.

Remember, the bracelet itself is far less important than the sentiment that it is given with. One glance at a friendship bracelet around your wrist, and fond thoughts of the friend who gave it to you are sure to follow.

CHAPTER 3

Mini-Blinds

As they walked home from the meeting together, Violet thought about how lucky she was to have Tigerlily as her best friend. Tigerlily was exciting and daring, and Violet always felt braver around her. She looked at her friendship bracelet and tucked in another loose string.

"Tigerlily," she said, "I don't need another friend, and I especially don't need to be friends with a Maple Scout."

"Me neither," said Tigerlily. "What do you want to do now?"

What Violet really wanted to do was get started on her friendship journal, but then she remembered that friendship is about give-and-take. And anyway, if she did something with Tigerlily now, she would have that much more to write in her journal later!

"I don't know," said Violet. "How about you?"

Tigerlily smiled. That's what she liked about Violet. She would almost always go along with whatever Tigerlily wanted to do.

"Let's go do something fun!" she said, and scampered off. Violet followed after her.

When Tigerlily came to the house where Violet lived, she didn't enter the small hole in the siding that led to Violet's home. Instead, she darted under the front door and into the humans' living room.

Violet was nervous. She didn't like being in the people part of the house during the day. Tigerlily didn't mind, though. She loved the feeling of carpet under her feet.

She climbed up the sofa and ran along the top of it. Then she took a flying leap to the window and landed on the slat of a mini-blind. "Come on up, Violet!" she shouted.

Violet looked up at Tigerlily. She was so high above the ground, Violet wasn't sure how to get herself up there. But as Tigerlily swung back and forth on the blind, Violet had to

admit that it *did* look like fun. She looked
around the room and listened. There was
no sign of any people.

Violet's nose twitched, but she gritted
her teeth and climbed up the sofa, then
ran across the top. The mini-blind still
looked very far away. But taking a deep
breath, Violet leaped as hard as she could
and just barely managed to grab on to the
blind. She was shaking all over as she

crawled along the slat to sit next to Tigerlily.

Violet was afraid to look down. It was
a long way to the floor. How in the world
were they going to get down again? They
might have to spend the rest of their lives
sitting on this blind!

Tigerlily did not seem uncomfortable
at all. She sat humming the Acorn Scout
song and swinging her legs back and forth

in time to the music. That made the whole blind sway. Violet began to feel seasick.

"What do you think Miss Poppy and her best friend used to do for fun?" Violet asked Tigerlily. "Do you think they ever played on mini-blinds?"

The thought of Miss Poppy doing anything of the sort made Violet laugh and forget where she was for a moment.

"She would probably get tangled up in the string!" Violet giggled. The blind shook with their laughter, but Violet didn't mind. She was starting to like it up here. Suddenly

she heard the creak of a door opening. "Human!" she squeaked.

Tigerlily reached for the blind's control wand and swung to a nearby lamp. She grabbed on to the lampshade, then leaped to the chair next to the lamp and scurried down to the floor. She looked behind her for Violet, but Violet was nowhere to be seen. "Hurry, Violet!" she hissed.

"Help!" Violet squeaked. Tigerlily had accidentally closed the blinds and Violet was trapped between the slats.

Tigerlily ran back to the window and jumped up to grab the wand. She twisted and twisted until the slats began to open. Violet tumbled out and bounced down

the slats all the way to the windowsill.
She landed for a moment, but then lost
her balance and bounced to the floor.

Violet stood up and straightened her
uniform. Her acorn cap had a small dent,
but otherwise there didn't seem to be any
permanent damage.
Then she
heard more
footsteps.
They were
getting closer.

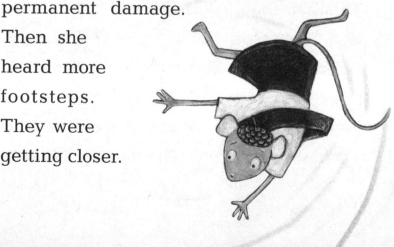

"Run!" squeaked Tigerlily. She and Violet scurried along the baseboard until they came to a mousehole. "In here!" said Tigerlily, about to duck in.

"Wait!" said Violet. "That's old Miss Pansy's house. She's even scarier than Miss Poppy! We can't go in there!"

The human's footsteps were in the room now. "We have no choice!" Tigerlily said, and dove through the hole. Violet was close behind.

Miss Pansy was in the middle of dusting her living room when Violet and Tigerlily tumbled in. "The nerve of you two!" she said, shaking her feather duster at them. "What is it with young mice today! In my day, we knew better than to barge into someone's home unannounced!"

"Sorry, Miss Pansy!" said Violet. Then she and Tigerlily climbed up the wall and squeezed through a tiny crack in the plaster. It led to a tunnel that eventually brought them to Violet's back door.

"See you tomorrow!" Tigerlily said. "Don't forget, we've got to come up with a plan for dealing with those Maple Scouts!" Then she ran through Violet's house and out the front door.

Violet was relieved when she sat down to work on her friendship journal. Sometimes being Tigerlily's friend could be TOO exciting. But still, Tigerlily was her best friend. And even if it wasn't the nicest bracelet, she loved the friendship bracelet Tigerlily had given her. Violet felt for the bracelet on her wrist, but there was nothing there. She jumped up and looked all around, but it was no use. Her friendship bracelet was gone!

MOUSE SCOUT HANDBOOK

Three Blind Mice: A Game About Trust

This game is designed for a troop of six mice but will work with any even number.

Before the game starts, set up an obstacle course. It can be as simple as a few chairs placed throughout a room. More complex courses could involve steps, jumps, or tunnels.

Once the course is set up, divide the mice into pairs. One mouse in each pair will put on a blindfold. The other mouse will act as a guide.

The guides will lead the blindfolded mice through the obstacle course.

Once the course has been completed, the mice will trade blindfolds.

The blindfolded mice must trust that their guides will safely take them through the obstacle course.

CHAPTER 4

❧

A Maple Scout!

Tigerlily took her time after leaving Violet's house. She thought about the friendship badge and how easy it was going to be to earn it. Friendship was one thing she was good at. And Violet was right: They didn't need anyone else, especially not a Maple Scout. Tigerlily touched her friendship bracelet and made a solemn vow to never speak to a Maple Scout.

Tigerlily was so busy thinking, she

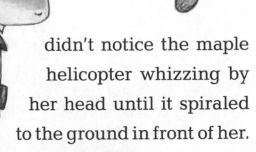

didn't notice the maple helicopter whizzing by her head until it spiraled to the ground in front of her. Tigerlily bent down to pick it up, when she heard a voice behind her squeak, "Hey! That's mine!"

Tigerlily turned around and found herself face to face with . . . a Maple Scout!

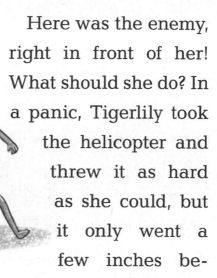

Here was the enemy, right in front of her! What should she do? In a panic, Tigerlily took the helicopter and threw it as hard as she could, but it only went a few inches before flopping to the ground. Tigerlily felt her ears prickle. The Maple Scout just laughed, picked up the helicopter, and expertly flung it. The helicopter soared high through the air and landed near the sandbox.

Tigerlily couldn't believe it. "How did you *do* that?" she asked.

"I'll show you!" the Maple Scout said.

He scampered off to the sandbox, and Tigerlily ran to catch up to him. Soon they were running neck and neck. Tigerlily lunged forward at the last second, just beating him to the sandbox. She picked up the helicopter and handed it to him.

"Thanks!" said the Maple Scout. He took the helicopter, held it for a moment, then very slowly threw it. The helicopter soared smoothly from his hand.

"See? You don't have to throw it so hard. It's all in the grip," he said, then trotted over to pick it up. When he got back to where Tigerlily was standing, he held out the helicopter and said, "Now *you* try!"

Tigerlily tried again—not quite so hard—and this time it went a little farther. She kept trying until she could throw it almost as well as the Maple Scout.

"Not bad for an Acorn Scout!" the Maple Scout laughed. Then he held out his hand and said, "My name is Thorn."

Tigerlily hesitated. He seemed nice enough, even if he was a Maple Scout. He didn't smell, and so far he hadn't eaten any worms. He was even polite. She shook his hand and said, "I'm Tigerlily!" Then she threw the helicopter

again. It soared through the sky, and slowly spiraled down near the birdbath. Tigerlily and Thorn ran side by side to pick it up.

When they reached the birdbath, they climbed up it, swam across, then climbed down again. They ran along the top of the swing set and slid down the slide. They climbed up the statue of the first mayor of Left Meadow, then dug tunnels in the

sandbox. Thorn and Tigerlily played in the park until it was almost dark.

"That was fun!" said Thorn. "Can we play again tomorrow?"

Tigerlily beamed. "Definitely!"

Tigerlily started to walk away, but Thorn shouted after her. "Wait!" he said. "We had to make friendship bracelets in Maple Scouts, and we're supposed to give one to a new friend. Can I give mine to you?"

Tigerlily's heart swelled. She reached into her pocket and pulled out her extra friendship bracelet and held it out for Thorn to see. "We did, too!" she said. They tied the bracelets on and examined them. The bracelet that Thorn made had loose strings everywhere. It looked a lot

like Tigerlily's. Thorn looked at Tigerlily and laughed. "I thought you Acorn Scouts were supposed to be good at crafts!"

Tigerlily gave him a playful shove and raced him to the park entrance. She won the race by a whisker.

That night, Tigerlily wrote all about Thorn in her friendship journal. She never would have believed it, but not only had she made a new friend, he was a *Maple* Scout!

MOUSE SCOUT HANDBOOK

A History of the Maple Scouts

The Maple Scouts were formed by a mouse named Alder, with the help of Hydrangea and Daisy, the original founders of the Mouse Scouts.

One day, Alder was searching for some food for his young family. He attempted to dislodge a piece of cheese from a mousetrap, but his timing was off, and—*snap!*—Alder's right arm was pinned in the trap.

Alder was sure he was a goner, but as luck would have it, a pair of Acorn Scouts found him. They managed to free Alder from the trap, then, using their first-aid skills, they made a splint for his arm out of toothpicks and a twist tie. One of the Scouts made a sling from her neck scarf. The Scouts helped Alder home and brought food for his family while he recovered.

Alder was so impressed, he made a point

of thanking Daisy and Hydrangea personally. He was intrigued with the concept of scouting and was surprised to learn that there was no such organization for boys.

Under the auspices of the Mouse Scouts, and with the encouragement of Hydrangea and Daisy, Alder formed the Maple Scouts. The Maple Scouts proved to be very popular. Soon a younger group, Dandelions, was

DANDELION   MAPLE   GOLDENROD

formed, which was the equivalent of Buttercups. As Maple Scouts grew older, Goldenrods, the equivalent to Sunflowers, was formed.

While Dandelions, Maple Scouts, and Goldenrods meet separately and earn their own badges, they often work in conjunction with Buttercups, Acorn Scouts, and Sunflowers.

CHAPTER 5

~ ❧ ~

Fractured Friendships

The next morning, Violet stopped by Tiger-lily's house on the way to the park. She had no idea what they could do to avoid working with the Maple Scouts, but she figured Tigerlily would have a plan. Tigerlily was always good at things like that. But when Violet got to Tigerlily's house, she wasn't there. Violet was puzzled. Where could Tigerlily be? Reluctantly, Violet decided to go to the park on her own.

Violet worried about Tigerlily all the way to the park. She felt her wrist where Tigerlily's friendship bracelet should have been. What if losing the friendship bracelet had caused something bad to happen? Maybe Tigerlily was in terrible danger!

Violet was so busy worrying about Tiger-lily that she didn't notice the maple helicopter whiz by her head until it almost hit her. As she bent down to pick it up, she heard a familiar voice.

"Hey, Violet!" Tigerlily called. "Throw it here!"

Violet felt the dark cloud of worry lift from her heart. She was so happy to hear Tigerlily's voice! But when Violet looked up, she immediately noticed that Tiger-lily was wearing *two* friendship bracelets. One was the neat one that she had given to Tigerlily, but the other one was sloppy, with loose strings hanging from it.

At first, Violet thought that Tigerlily must have kept her extra friendship bracelet, but that didn't make sense. Then Violet spotted . . . a Maple Scout! But why was Tigerlily smiling at him? And why was he wearing a sloppy-looking friendship bracelet just like the one Tigerlily had given to her? It could only mean one thing:

Tigerlily had made friends with a Maple Scout!

Violet opened her mouth in disbelief, but Tigerlily didn't seem to notice.

"Violet, this is my new friend, Thorn!" Tigerlily said. "He knows how to make a canoe, and he's going to show me. Want to come down to the stream with us?"

Violet did not want to go with them. She

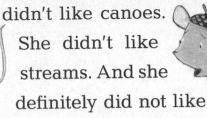

didn't like canoes. She didn't like streams. And she definitely did not like Maple Scouts. Violet felt her nose tingle, and she could feel tears starting to well up in her eyes. "I'm sorry, I'm busy!" she blurted out, and ran in the other direction.

Violet couldn't believe it. Tigerlily was *her* best friend. What was Tigerlily doing making friends with a *Maple* Scout! It wasn't fair. She made a solemn vow to never speak to Tigerlily again.

Violet was in tears by the time she met up with the other Acorn Scouts at the sandbox.

They were hard at work coloring pieces
of cardboard. Hyacinth was telling everyone what to do, and no one seemed very
happy.

"There you are, Violet," Hyacinth said.
"I decided that we should make protest
signs for our next Mouse Scout meeting.
Join in! Make sure that it is clear from the
sign that Maple Scouts are *not* welcome
at our meeting. Don't use too many colors,
and don't be messy."

Violet sat down and picked up a crayon. She drew a maple helicopter with a line through it. She was quite pleased with herself.

Hyacinth looked at Petunia's sign. It read NO MAPEL SCOUTS! Hyacinth pointed at it and laughed. "Petunia, I can't believe you don't know how to spell," she said.

Petunia frowned. "Your sign isn't that great, either," she replied. Hyacinth glared at her. Petunia picked up her sign and marched out of the park.

"I brought some crackers, if any-one wants some," Cricket said, trying to change the subject. She spread the crackers out on a tissue.

Junebug picked up a cracker and examined it. "I can't eat these! They have caraway seeds in them. You *know* that caraway seeds give me a rash."

Cricket sighed and hung her head. She had tried to bring a snack that Junebug would like. "Everything gives you a rash," she muttered.

Junebug gave Cricket a pointed look. "I can't help it if my system is more sensitive than yours. It must be nice to be able to eat everything in sight." Junebug picked up her sign and followed Petunia.

Cricket gulped. She wasn't sure, but she thought that Junebug might have insulted her. She looked at her cracker. She didn't even feel like eating it anymore. She packed up her crackers and started for home.

"Where's Tigerlily?" Hyacinth asked Violet. "I thought she would be here by now. It was her idea to come up with a plan so we didn't have to work with the Maple Scouts."

Violet told her about Tigerlily and the Maple Scout. When she was finished, she burst into tears all over again.

Hyacinth patted her on the shoulder. "I don't know what we are going to do, Violet. This friendship badge is tearing us apart."

Violet smiled at Hyacinth through her tears. At least she still had *one* friend in the Acorn Scouts!

Mouse Mime:
An Exercise in Communication

In every friendship there can be times of misunderstanding. It can be easy to leap to conclusions without paying attention to what your friend is saying.

This game will help mice to pay attention to what their friends may be thinking or feeling—without their friend saying a single word!

Have one mouse be "It." She will stand in front of the other mice. The troop leader will pose a general question to the mouse who is "It." She may respond using only gestures and facial expressions. Each mouse in the troop will then ask a follow-up question. Guesses to the answer may be made at any time.

Some sample questions:

- What Mouse Scout badge would you most like to earn?
- What was your happiest time?
- What qualities make a good friend?

Scouts will not only have fun putting their dramatic skills to the test, they will also learn to be more attentive friends.

What do you want to do when you grow up?

What is your favorite time of day?

What makes a good friend?

(Ballet dancer)

(Morning)

(Be helpful and listen)

CHAPTER 6

A Surprising Friend

Days went by, and the Acorn Scouts barely spoke to each other. Violet avoided Tigerlily, but Tigerlily hardly noticed—she was too busy with Thorn.

Violet spent her time sitting in the park, remembering when all of the Mouse Scouts were still friends. She felt her wrist where Tigerlily's bracelet should have

been and wondered if she would ever have a friend again. As she sat there, the sprinkler system in the park came on, drenching her. *It figures*, Violet thought. *Nothing in this world is right.*

Violet stood up and shook off as much water as she could. She wandered over to a rock by the swing set, hoping to dry herself off in the sun. But when she got to the rock, someone was already sitting there. It was Miss Poppy!

"Oh, hello, Violet," Miss Poppy said. "Isn't it a lovely day?"

For a moment, Violet was speechless. She had never had a conversation with Miss Poppy outside of a Mouse Scout meeting. In fact, she had a hard time believing that Miss Poppy *existed* outside of Mouse Scouts. But here she was. And she was even being friendly.

Violet wiped her eyes. "Oh, Miss Poppy! The 'Make Friends' badge is the hardest badge we have ever worked on. No one is speaking to anyone, and Tigerlily is friends with a Maple Scout! I am never going to speak to her again!"

Miss Poppy smiled and motioned for Violet to sit down. Violet was nervous, but she did as Miss Poppy asked.

"Violet, can I ask you a question?" Miss Poppy said.

Violet gulped and blinked back her tears. "I guess so," she replied in a quavering voice.

"What is your favorite kind of cheese?" Miss Poppy asked.

Violet didn't know how Miss Poppy could talk about cheese at a time like this. She was too upset to even think about cheese, but she answered anyway.

"Cheddar," Violet said.

"Is that the *only* kind of cheese you like?" Miss Poppy asked.

"Of course not!" said Violet. "I like Gouda, and Brie, and Swiss, and—" Violet forgot about how upset she was. Suddenly she felt very hungry. "Miss Poppy, are we going to have a snack?"

But Miss Poppy continued to speak. "I was just thinking, that even if cheddar is your favorite cheese, sometimes it can be nice to try something else," Miss Poppy said. "It doesn't mean you like cheddar *less*. Do you understand what I am trying to say?"

Violet still wondered why Miss Poppy was talking about cheese, but she nodded just the same. Everyone she knew liked lots of different cheeses. Except for Junebug, of course.

Miss Poppy smiled back. "Now that I think of it, a snack WOULD be nice." She rummaged in her bag and pulled out a small piece of cheese. She split it in two pieces and handed one to Violet. Violet took a bite. It was Stilton, and it was delicious.

"Thank you, Miss Poppy," Violet said.

"You are welcome, Violet. I'm glad we had this talk," Miss Poppy replied with a smile. Then her smile vanished, and she looked more like regular old Miss Poppy. "Now, don't forget. You have badge requirements to be working on. I will see you at the next meeting, *with* the Maple Scouts."

Later that evening as Violet wrote in her friendship journal, she thought about what Miss Poppy had said about cheese. Suddenly it made sense! Miss Poppy hadn't really been talking about cheese at all. She was talking about *friendship*. Just because Tigerlily had made a new friend didn't mean that Violet was any less important to her. Violet was Tigerlily's cheddar! And Thorn was— Violet tried to imagine what kind of cheese Thorn would be. She held her pencil to her nose and thought. Then she remembered the time Tigerlily had given her a stinky piece of cheese. Tigerlily didn't seem to mind it, but Violet hadn't cared for it at all!

"Thorn is *Limburger!*" Violet said with a satisfied giggle.

Then Violet grew wistful. *Tigerlily is* my *cheddar, too*, she thought. She

wondered about Miss Poppy and who *her* cheddar was. Maybe it was the long-lost friend that she and Tigerlily had giggled about the day they played on the miniblinds. She felt her wrist and wished she hadn't lost Tigerlily's friendship bracelet. And then it occurred to her: She knew exactly where she had lost the bracelet!

MOUSE SCOUT HANDBOOK

Making and Keeping a Friendship Journal

A friendship journal is a wonderful way to keep track of and celebrate your friendships. You may use any notebook you like, or you may make your own. (Instructions for making a journal can be found in the "Make a Difference" section of this handbook.)

When you have your notebook, divide it into two sections. In the front section, write a page about each of your friends.

A sample page may look like this:

My friend's name is: _____

We have known each other since: _____

This is how we met: _____

_____

_____

Her birthday is: _____

Her favorite color is: _____

I like her because: _____

_____

_____

_____

We have these things in common: _____

_____

_____

_____

Some fun facts about my friend: _____

_____

_____

_____

You may also include pictures or drawings of your friends and things that remind you of them.

In the second section, keep a daily diary of your friendship activities.

CHAPTER 7

Cheddar and Limburger

Tigerlily spent the week building a canoe with Thorn. The Maple Scouts had made one out of birch bark for a badge a few months before, so Thorn knew what to do. First they found some birch bark. Thorn showed Tigerlily how to fold it up so that it was shaped like a canoe. Then they used pine needles to sew the front and the back edges together. Tigerlily was suddenly glad that Violet had taught her

how to sew. Who knew that sewing would actually come in handy?!

When the canoe was finished, they found some sticks. Thorn showed Tigerlily how to carve them into paddles. Finally they were ready to put the canoe in the water.

On the morning of the Mouse Scout meeting, Tigerlily

and Thorn met at the stream. They dragged their canoe to the edge of the water. Tigerlily got in first and steadied the canoe with her paddle. Then Thorn pushed the canoe away from the bank and jumped in.

The current was strong, and they glided quickly down the stream. Tigerlily loved feeling the wind on her ears. Then she saw a group of rocks up ahead. She tried to steer with her paddle, but they were moving too fast. They were going to crash! There was only one thing to do. "ABANDON SHIP!" she shouted.

Tigerlily and Thorn jumped out of the canoe into the water. Then they swam as hard as they could for the edge of the stream. They pulled themselves onto the bank just in time to watch the canoe bounce through the rocks.

Tigerlily's heart sank. They had worked so hard on the canoe. If Violet were here, she would be in tears. Tigerlily felt close to tears herself. She blinked and looked at Thorn.

"Don't worry," he said. "We can always make another one."

Tigerlily smiled and stretched out to dry in the sun. It was nice being friends with a Maple Scout.

Tigerlily's thoughts turned to the Acorn Scouts. Some friends *they* were. She had

hardly seen them since their last meeting. Hyacinth and Petunia had ignored her in the park. Junebug and Cricket had walked the other way when they saw her coming. And she hadn't seen Violet for a few days. Tigerlily felt a lump in her throat. Then she felt a little mad. They were supposed to be working on the "Make Friends" badge together, but there wasn't much *together* in sight!

"I'm glad you're coming to our Mouse Scout meeting today," Tigerlily said to Thorn. "You might be my only friend there!"

Thorn laughed. "The Maple Scouts aren't happy about it, either," he said. "But they'll get over it." He took a piece of cheese from his backpack and handed some to Tigerlily.

"Holy moly, Gorgonzoli!" Tigerlily said.

Thorn gave her a funny look. "It's called Gorgonzola," he said.

"I know," Tigerlily said, "but it didn't fit the rhyme." Tigerlily was surprised. She never had to explain cheese rhymes to Violet.

"That's silly," said Thorn.

"Yeah, I guess you're right," said Tigerlily. But she didn't think it was silly at all.
She had a sharp pang of missing Violet.

Thorn interrupted Tigerlily's thoughts.
"Race you up that tree!" he said, and
jumped up. Tigerlily forgot about Violet
and ran after Thorn.

They raced neck and neck to the tree,
then climbed up to the very top. Thorn

jumped across to a branch on the next tree. Tigerlily was standing right behind him, and the bounce Thorn made when he jumped almost made her slip!

She grabbed on to the branch
and held tight while she caught
her breath. She thought again about
Violet. Tigerlily had been so proud of her
the day they played on the mini-blinds.
Violet had been fearless!

Suddenly it seemed important to see
Violet before the Mouse Scout meeting.
Tigerlily wanted to tell her that Maple
Scouts were okay. But most of all, she
wanted to tell Violet that she was still her
best friend. She only hoped that Violet felt
the same way.

Tigerlily jumped down from branch

to branch, then scrambled down the tree trunk to the ground. She looked back up to the treetop where Thorn was still playing.

"Hey, Thorn, I've got to go!" she called. "I'll see you at the meeting!"

MOUSE SCOUT HANDBOOK

Mouse Scout Friendships
Lost and Found

Through the Mouse Scouts, many lifelong friendships are formed. But it is not always smooth sailing. Even best friends can hit rough seas and stormy weather, as these stories will illustrate.

Trillium and Bud: Alder's son Bud was one of the first Maple Scouts. Because the Maple Scouts were still catching on, they often had joint meetings with Acorn Scouts. It was at one of those meetings that Bud met Daisy's daughter Trillium. The two were inseparable. As often happens with young friends, though, they went their separate ways when Trillium graduated from Sunflower Scouts and Bud from the Goldenrods. Trillium never forgot her love for scouting, and after graduating from Maus University, she became an Acorn Scout leader. One of her first activities was a joint meeting with the Maple Scouts. Trillium was surprised to find the Maple Scout leader was none other than her old friend Bud! They quickly rekindled their friendship . . . which before long turned to love.

TRILLIUM AND BUD

Azalea and Blossom had been best friends ever since Buttercups. They shared a love of ballet and were excited when it was finally time to work on a dance badge. That excitement soon turned to heartbreak, at least for Azalea. Blossom was chosen for the lead in the pageant, while Azalea was asked to be a stagehand. Blossom was so thrilled to be the star that she had little time for Azalea, and she failed to see that Azalea's feelings were hurt. The day before the performance, Blossom

AZALEA AND BLOSSOM

twisted her ankle while running from a cat. She would be unable to perform. Azalea offered to stand in for Blossom. She performed beautifully, and even Blossom had to admit that Azalea had been perfect. At the end of the performance, Azalea called Blossom up to the stage, and they both took a bow.

⟳

Holly and Jasmine never liked each other. They had very different personalities and couldn't see eye to eye. But in a twist of fate, the two mice were separated from their troop during a hike. There was a sudden snowstorm, and they needed to find shelter. Holly discovered an abandoned chipmunk hole, and Jasmine reluctantly followed her. While they waited out the storm, their coldness toward each other gradually thawed. Holly was surprised to learn that Jasmine was actually very shy. Jasmine was surprised by Holly's plucky sense of humor. By the time the storm had ended and the Scouts were reunited with their troop, they had become the best of friends!

HOLLY AND JASMINE

CHAPTER 8

Daring Violet

Violet had just enough time before the Mouse Scout meeting to search for her friendship bracelet. Maybe, if she found it, everything would be all right again between her and Tigerlily.

Violet stood at the edge of the humans' living room. She listened carefully to make sure there was no sounds of humans.

Satisfied that there weren't any people around, Violet took a deep breath. Then she tiptoed through the room as fast as she could. When she got to the window, she looked up. Sure enough, her friendship bracelet was stuck on the seventh slat of the mini-blind!

Violet wondered what to do next. With Tigerlily's encouragement, she had climbed up the mini-blinds the other day. But Tigerlily wasn't here now. Violet sniffed. She would just have to do it herself!

Violet climbed up the sofa and ran along the top of it. She sped up, and when she reached the edge of the sofa, she took a flying leap toward the window. Violet landed squarely on the slat of the mini-blind. She held her breath and looked down. She had jumped too far! Her friendship bracelet was three slats below her.

Violet grabbed on to the wand and shimmied down. When she reached the slat that the friendship bracelet was on, she stretched out as far as she could. Violet was just able to grab the bracelet. Her heart swelled! She had it!

Suddenly the wand swung away from the blind, and Violet nearly lost her grip. It swung back and forth a few more times before finally coming to a stop. Violet looked down. She couldn't believe how high above the ground she was. For a moment, she felt dizzy. Somehow, she was going to have to get herself down. She felt herself slip a little on the wand. *Uh-oh!* she thought, then she pushed against the wall before losing her grip altogether and falling to the ground.

Violet sat up and checked herself for injuries. Other than another small dent in her acorn cap, she seemed to be fine. She quickly tied the friendship bracelet around her wrist. Then she straightened her uniform and looked up at the blind. She had fallen quite a distance, but she had survived! She touched the friendship bracelet on  her wrist. Tigerlily would be so proud!

Violet was thinking about how she would describe her adventure to Tigerlily when she heard footsteps . . . human footsteps! She froze for a moment. She knew she was near Miss Pansy's doorway, but it had been one thing to face Miss Pansy with Tigerlily; it would be another thing to face her alone! The footsteps were coming closer and closer until Violet had no choice. She ran as fast as she could to Miss Pansy's doorway, but when she got there, she found another problem. Miss Pansy's doorway had been blocked with steel wool!

"Oh no!" Violet cried. Steel wool in a doorway meant that humans knew there were mice living there, too. Violet tried to think of what to do. Maybe she should just run out the front door. But it was too risky.

Violet flattened herself against the baseboard and tried to be invisible. She shut her eyes and listened as the 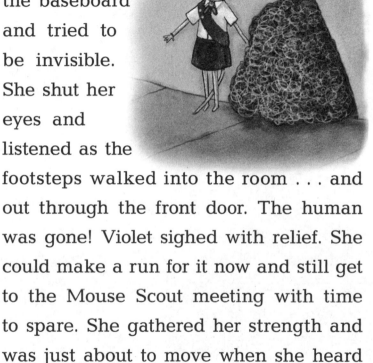 footsteps walked into the room . . . and out through the front door. The human was gone! Violet sighed with relief. She could make a run for it now and still get to the Mouse Scout meeting with time to spare. She gathered her strength and was just about to move when she heard a new noise. From behind the steel wool, she heard a faint squeak. It could only be Miss Pansy!

MOUSE SCOUT HANDBOOK

Face Your Fears!

Everyone is afraid of something, no matter how brave they think they are. This activity will help Scouts realize that by looking at their fears from a different perspective, they might not seem so bad after all!

Here's how to play:

- Have each Scout write down something she is afraid of on a slip of paper.

- Place the papers in an acorn cap.

- Shake the cap to mix up the paper slips.

- Have each Scout draw one slip of paper from the cap.

- The Scouts can take turns acting out the fear written on their slip of paper.

Without poking fun at the fear itself, Scouts should offer humorous examples of how the fear may be faced.

CHAPTER 9

Mouse Scouts to the Rescue!

I've got to save her! Violet thought. She started pulling at the steel wool with her hands, but it was sharp and prickly, and there was just too much of it.

"It's no use," Violet cried. "I can't do this myself."

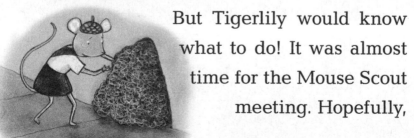

But Tigerlily would know what to do! It was almost time for the Mouse Scout meeting. Hopefully,

Tigerlily would be on her way there. Violet dashed out the door.

Tigerlily was almost at Violet's front door. She just had to talk to Violet before the Mouse Scout meeting. She was trying to think of what to say when Violet came running around a corner and crashed into her.

"Violet!" Tigerlily cried. "I was just coming to find you! I'm sorry—"

"There's no time for that now," Violet interrupted. "Miss Pansy is in trouble. We've got to save her!"

Violet explained to Tigerlily about the steel wool. Tigerlily thought hard. She didn't have any of her emergency tools with her. Even her pockets were empty. Tigerlily knew enough about steel wool to know that she and Violet were no match for it. "Violet, we're going to need more help. Let's go find the other Scouts!"

They started running to the Left Meadow Elementary School when—*bam!* Tigerlily crashed into Thorn. Violet was right behind Tigerlily, and— *bam!*—she crashed into Tigerlily.

"Tigerlily!" Thorn cried. "Where did you run off to? I thought we were going to the meeting—"

"Follow us!" Tigerlily interrupted. "We need more help!"

The three Scouts ran to the Left Meadow Elementary School. When they got there, they found a standoff.

Hyacinth, Petunia, Junebug, and Cricket were blocking the entry to the Left Meadow Elementary School cafeteria. Each Scout was holding one of the signs they had made in the park. Facing them were five Maple Scouts.

Hyacinth began chanting, "Hey, hey, ho, ho! Maple Scouts have got to go!" and the other Acorns joined in.

The Maple Scouts shouted back, "Ho, ho, hey, hey! Maple Scouts are here to STAY!"

"Excuse me, everyone!" Violet said, but no one was listening. She tried again and even waved her arms, but they all kept shouting.

"Times of emergency call for emergency measures," Tigerlily said. She took out her emergency whistle and put it to her mouth. *THWEEEEEEEET!*

Everyone stopped chanting and turned to Tigerlily.

"We need help!" Tigerlily explained the situation.

"But what can we do?" asked Hyacinth. "Steel wool is almost impossible to deal with. We can't chew it, and it is too sharp and prickly to pull with our hands. We're just little mice, after all."

Thorn walked over and stood next to Tigerlily. "Of course we can help," he said. "If we all work together, we can do anything. We're more than mice. We're Mouse Scouts!"

We're MOUSE SCOUTS!

The Acorn Scouts looked at him in awe. He sounded just like Tigerlily.

"Thorn is right!" said Tigerlily. "It doesn't matter if you're an Acorn or a Maple. We're *all* Mouse Scouts! And we have a job to do!"

The six Acorn Scouts and the six Maple Scouts ran back to the house, with Tigerlily, Thorn, and Violet leading the way. When they got to the house, they squeezed under the front door and raced to the living room. Violet showed them the steel wool, and they got to work.

They started to tug at the steel wool, but it was too difficult. Tigerlily took off her neck scarf and wrapped it around her hands, which made it easier to pull at the steel wool. Thorn took off his cap and used it as a glove. He and Tigerlily worked hard, but the steel wool was not budging.

Violet looked at Thorn and then looked at the protest signs. She picked one up and ripped the sign from the toothpick it was taped to. Then, using the tooth-pick, she started to pry at the steel wool. Hyacinth and Petunia did the same.

"It's getting looser!" said Cricket.

"Watch out for your eyes!" cried Junebug. "A scratch from the metal could cause permanent damage!"

"Not to worry!" said one of the other Maple Scouts. He grabbed the paper from the signs and quickly fashioned some visors. Junebug gazed at him in amazement as he handed them out. She had no idea that Maple Scouts could be so safety-minded.

Two more Maple
Scouts joined in,
pushing at the steel
wool from the side.
They heard a horrible
scratchy scraping
noise, and finally the
steel wool gave way.
The Scouts cheered.

When they finally stopped cheering, it was very quiet. *Too* quiet. Were they too late? Was Miss Pansy even there? All twelve Scouts held their breath until Miss Pansy peeked around the doorway. For a moment, Violet was afraid that she would yell at them, but then Miss Pansy smiled broadly.

"My heroes! If there weren't so many of you, I'd invite you all in for cookies and tea!" she said.

"Thank you, Miss Pansy," Tigerlily answered. "But now that you're safe, we've got to be going. We are late for our Mouse Scout meeting."

At that, Miss Pansy got a dreamy look

in her eyes. "I remember *my* Mouse Scout days. Some of the happiest times in my life."

"Miss Pansy?" Violet asked. "Would you like to come to our Celebration of Friendship?"

"I would love to!" said Miss Pansy.

Meanwhile, in the basement of the Left Meadow Elementary School, Miss Poppy paced back and forth. She knew the

Acorns were not happy with the idea of working with the Maple Scouts. *Well!* she thought. *I will just have to talk to them about opening their minds and being accepting of others.* She steeled herself and looked at the clock. *But if they are much later,* she thought, *I may just have to send them back to Buttercups. And I'll make sure it is straight back to Dandelions for those Maple Scouts!*

Just then the Acorn Scouts and the Maple Scouts all tumbled into the Left Meadow Elementary School basement together. And every single one of them was laughing as if they had been friends forever.

Miss Poppy blew her emergency whistle, and with the slightest of smiles said,

"Quiet, Scouts! We have a celebration to plan!"

125

MOUSE SCOUT HANDBOOK

The Kindness Challenge

Kindness is one of the most important virtues a Mouse Scout can have. Sometimes it is easy to be kind, and sometimes it takes just a little bit of effort. Having a Kindness Challenge is a fun way to understand the importance and benefits of kindness. Here's how it works!

Designate a week for your Kindness Challenge. Ask your fellow Scouts to commit themselves to performing at least one kind deed every day. It may be as simple as helping another mouse pick up some sunflower seeds she has dropped. It might be a greater kindness, such as helping someone out of a tough situation. Of course, you may always do more than one kind thing in a day, but that does not mean you may skip the next day! Keep track of your kind acts by making a chart.

	MONDAY	TUESDAY	WEDNESDAY	THURSDAY	FRIDAY	SATURDAY	SUNDAY
A KIND THING I DID	Helped a Buttercup get to her meeting	Left a flower for my neighbor	Moved a rock out of a chipmunk hole	Gave directions to a lost ladybug	Made cheese croissants for the old mouse home	Did not step on an ant	Visited my neighbor
ANOTHER KIND THING I DID	Brought a blueberry to Mr. Conifer	Smiled at my neighbor (who I don't know)	Helped a fly out of a spider web	Helped Mr. Viburnum stack a pile of acorns			
ONE MORE KIND THING I DID	Picked up some trash	Made friends with my neighbor					

At the end of your Kindness Challenge Week, Scouts may bring their charts to their Mouse Scout meeting and share them. You will no doubt be impressed and inspired by all of the kind things your fellow Mouse Scouts have done.

Being kind to others not only brightens their day, it can also open the door to friendship!

CHAPTER 10

A Celebration of Friendship

By the time the day of the Celebration of Friendship arrived, the Acorn Scouts and Maple Scouts were such good friends that Violet could hardly remember why they had been against them in the first place. Thorn's friend Thistle was very quiet, but Violet thought he had great potential.

Cricket and Weevil hit it off immediately. Hornet was as sly and funny as Petunia, while Sycamore was as handsome as Hyacinth was beautiful. Junebug found a soul mate in Woodruff, who had an allergy to dust mites.

Achoo!

Hyacinth and Sycamore put the finishing touches on the decorations for the celebration, while Cricket and Weevil put out the snacks.

Thorn and Thistle helped Tigerlily and Violet set up some tables and chairs, while Junebug and Woodruff made name tags. Finally everything was ready.

"You've done very well, Scouts!" said Miss Poppy. She turned and smiled almost shyly at the Maple Scout leader: a dapper mouse named Mr. Spruce.

"This will be a true celebration of friendship. Let the festivities begin."

The Scouts all enjoyed a game of pin
the wings on the bumblebee, and then

Thorn and Tigerlily helped teach the
Acorn Scouts how to throw maple heli-
copters like a boomerang.

Violet was enjoying herself, but she kept watching the door, waiting for Miss Pansy to arrive. She had seen her a few times since the steel wool incident, and each time Miss Pansy seemed nicer and nicer. Violet was looking forward to introducing her to Miss Poppy. They both seemed like they could use a friend.

Finally the door opened and Miss Pansy walked in. She was smiling when she came in, but then she froze, and her smile changed to a frown. Violet turned to see who she was looking at. It was Miss Poppy—and she had the same unhappy look on her face as Miss Pansy!

"YOU!" they both said at the same time. Violet gulped. Something terrible and unexpected was happening. She had no idea that Miss Pansy and Miss Poppy even knew each other.

Violet looked at Tigerlily. "Do you think Miss Pansy could be Miss Poppy's long-lost friend?" Violet whispered.

"They sure don't seem like friends now," Tigerlily answered.

"Are you here to apologize at long last?" Miss Poppy said to Miss Pansy.

"Me? Apologize to YOU?" said Miss Pansy. "You're the one who thought it would be such a great idea to go down that rabbit hole."

"Rabbit hole?" Miss Poppy shouted.

"What rabbit hole? I'm talking about that tea you made with poison ivy!"

"That was an honest mistake," Miss Pansy spluttered. "I thought it was *mint!*"

"Clearly, you did not study your *Mouse Scout Handbook* carefully," Miss Poppy said. "It was a week before I stopped looking like a chipmunk."

The two of them stared at each other for a long time. Violet and Tigerlily felt helpless. Then Miss Poppy's face began to soften.

"Of course, I did make new friends that week," Miss Poppy said. "A chipmunk even showed me his secret stash of beechnuts!"

Miss Pansy's mouth twitched. "I remember him. He was so heartbroken when your swelling went down and he realized you were a mouse!"

Suddenly they were both laughing and hugging.

"I can't believe we let ever such a silly thing come between us!" Miss Poppy said.

Violet and Tigerlily breathed a sigh of relief. "I'll never let anything or anyone come between us again," Violet said to Tigerlily.

"Me either," said Tigerlily.

MOUSE SCOUT HANDBOOK

Being a Good Friend

The best way to *make* a friend is to *be* a friend. Here are some of the things a good friend does:

- A good friend is a good listener.
- A good friend pays attention to how her friends feel.
- A good friend doesn't say mean things or hurt anyone's feelings.

- A good friend helps her friends solve problems.
- A good friend gives compliments to her friends.
- A good friend is trustworthy.
- A good friend can disagree without hurting her friends.
- A good friend lets her friends be themselves.
- A good friend is caring.
- A good friend is kind.

Are *you* a good friend?

The Badge Ceremony

MOUSE SCOUT HANDBOOK

THE "MAKE FRIENDS" BADGE

To earn this badge, you must complete the following requirements:

1. Make two friendship bracelets.

2. Reach out to make new friends.

3. Give one bracelet to a good friend, and one bracelet to a new friend.

4. Keep a friendship journal.

5. Be a good friend.

6. Help your troop prepare a Celebration of Friendship.

MOUSE SCOUT BADGES

Sow It and Grow It

Mouse Scout Heritage

Fun and Foraging

Make a Difference

Baking with Seeds

Take Flight

Dramatics

Signs of Fall

First Aid

Winter Safety

Predator Awareness

Camp Out

Flower Fashions

Weaving with Grass

The Night Sky

Friendship

THE ACORN SCOUT SONG

Melody by Frank Fighera

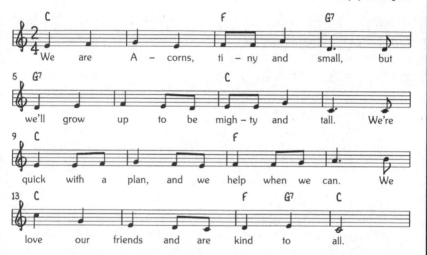

We are A - corns, ti - ny and small, but we'll grow up to be migh - ty and tall. We're quick with a plan, and we help when we can. We love our friends and are kind to all.

MOUSE SCOUT FRIENDSHIP SONG

Melody by Frank Fighera

Mouse Scouts, Mouse Scouts, smart and cle - ver. Strong as Roque - fort, sharp as

ched - dar. We work hard to make the world

bet - ter. Mouse Scouts, Mouse Scouts, friends for - ev - er!

Sarah Dillard was briefly a Brownie and a Junior Scout. She fondly remembers making macaroni necklaces and, less fondly, one horrible camping trip when she had to eat the worst oatmeal ever. On the brighter side, Sarah studied art at Wheaton College and illustration at the Rhode Island School of Design. In addition to the Mouse Scouts series, she is the creator of picture books such as *Perfectly Arugula* and *Extraordinary Warren*. She lives in Waitsfield, Vermont, with her husband. Visit Sarah at sarahdillard.com.

The Smallest Scouts
with the biggest hearts!

Do you want to earn YOUR Mouse Scout badge?

Join Violet, Tigerlily, Hyacinth, Petunia,

Junebug, and Cricket on all of their adventures!

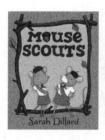